W

THE POOH
SKETCHBOOK

E.H. Shepard

THE POOH
SKETCHBOOK

Edited by
Brian Sibley

Roy Strong

E. P. DUTTON · NEW YORK

First published in the U.S.A. 1984 by E. P. Dutton, Inc.
2 Park Avenue, New York, N.Y. 10016

First published in Great Britain 1982
by Methuen Children's Books Ltd
11 New Fetter Lane, London EC4P 4EE

Designed by Zena Flax Associates.

Phototypeset by Tradespools Limited, Frome, Somerset.
Printed in Great Britain by BAS Printers Limited, Over Wallop,
Hampshire

ISBN 0-525-44084-4
COBE
10 9 8 7 6 5 4 3 2 1

CONTENTS

FOREWORD

E.H. Shepard's illustrations to A.A. Milne's *Pooh* stories form
without doubt one of the great classics of children's book illustration.
It is important to understand, however, how remarkable that is, for
Shepard's success as an illustrator was not based on that technical
power of draughtsmanship we see in the work of artists such as
Rackham. We do not go with him for a prolonged journey of the eye
as we do with the great masters of drawing. His illustrations are
classics for a wholly different reason. Our approach must be through
the eyes of childhood, for Shepard's Pooh, Piglet, Eeyore and Tigger
cast their compulsive spell because the artist only ever makes them
but very slightly removed from the stuffed toys on the nursery shelf.
Whereas Beatrix Potter's animals are almost transformed into furry
occupants of the same domain, in the case of Shepard the journey is
made in precisely the opposite direction. Their relationship to the
ephemeral art of *Punch* is also abundantly clear. There is a slightness
to them, a delightful, rapid, thrown-off quality, particularly in the
many thumbnail sketches dotted through the text. This is an adult
aesthetic judgement and one which in no way affects how one saw
them as a child and how young readers still see and respond to them.
Shepard's genius lay surely in being able to match exactly the mood
of Milne's texts which have a similar and complementary rambling
quality. A less whimsical artist would have upset the balance. As it is,
writer and illustrator were perfectly allied in a curiously English way,
achieving thereby one of the great classics of childhood literature.

Roy Strong

The pictures in this book have been chosen from the collection of original
sketches bequeathed in 1969 by Ernest Shepard to the Victoria and Albert
Museum. The annotations on the pictures were made by the artist when he
presented them to the Museum and the page references which he gave refer
to the first published editions of the books.

For my Mother and Father
who first introduced me to
The World of Pooh

B.S.

The Editor gratefully acknowledges the help and co-operation so generously given him in the preparation of this book by the Department of Prints and Drawings at the Victoria & Albert Muscum; Miss Joyce I. Whalley, Librarian at the Victoria & Albert Museum; and the Staff of the British Museum.
Sketches on the top left of page 14, the bottom right of page 25, the bottom left of page 55, the top left of page 56 and the whole of page 63 copyright © 1979 by Lloyds Bank Ltd and Colin Anthony Richards, Executors of the Estate of E.H. Shepard, rest copyright © 1982 Lloyds Bank Ltd and Colin Anthony Richards, Executors of the Estate of E.H. Shepard, and the E.H. Shepard Trust.

INTRODUCTION

The collaboration of writer A.A. Milne and illustrator E.H. Shepard
has proved one of the most successful partnerships of its kind, yet it
was a partnership which nearly didn't come about.

Alan Alexander Milne (1882–1956), already an established
playwright and essayist, began writing for children in 1923 when he
wrote what was to become his most famous poem, 'Vespers'. Later
the same year he contributed a second poem, 'The Dormouse and the
Doctor', to the magazine *Merry-go-Round*, and was encouraged to try
and write a book of verse. This he did, entitling it *When We Were Very
Young*. *Punch*, of which Milne was a former Assistant Editor, decided
to preview extracts from the book, and fellow essayist and verse-
writer E.V. Lucas recommended E.H. Shepard as a possible
illustrator.

Ernest Howard Shepard (1879–1976) had been illustrating books
for twenty years, and had contributed regular cartoons to *Punch* since
1907. Milne disliked Shepard's style, however, and was not
impressed by the suggestion from E.V. Lucas that Shepard should
illustrate *When We Were Very Young*. Undaunted, Lucas continued to
promote Shepard, and the artist prepared some specimen drawings
for Milne to see. Milne was immediately won over, and the
publication in *Punch* of his verses and Shepard's decorations during
the first six months of 1924 received an enthusiastic reception from
the public. *When We Were Very Young*, with many more poems and
illustrations, was published in book form by Methuen later the same
year.

Several of the verses were about Milne's son, Christopher Robin,
and the author next began a series of stories about Christopher and
his nursery toys. When the book was completed, there was no
argument about who should illustrate it – it had to be Shepard.
Winnie-the-Pooh was published in 1926, and was followed, in 1927, by
a second book of verses, *Now We Are Six*, and, in 1928, by Pooh's
further exploits, *The House at Pooh Corner*. With his illustrations to
these books – and those which he later made for Kenneth Grahame's
The Wind in the Willows – Shepard won lasting and justified fame.

Shepard's talent lay in his gentleness as an observer of life, and in
the accuracy and precision of his draughtsmanship; qualities clearly
seen in the pictures in this book. Look, for example, at the picture of
Pooh and Piglet struggling against the wind on that blusterous day
'when something Oo occurred' (page 85), or at that of Eeyore
gloomily contemplating his reflection in the stream (page 35). There
is Shepard's genius.

Before working on his illustrations to the Pooh books, Shepard visited Milne and his family at Cotchford Farm at Hartfield in Sussex. He met Christopher and the toys and was taken by Milne to the various locations in and around Ashdown Forest where the stories were set. Shepard made numerous sketches and studies of trees and landscapes, and in using these naturalistic settings as backgrounds for the fantasies, he gave a convincing realism to the books.

Shepard worked from rough sketches and life studies and then prepared a detailed pencil drawing; the back of this drawing would be rubbed over with pencil until it was covered with graphite; then the drawing would be laid graphite side down on art-card and retraced, so as to leave a light image which could be followed in producing the final ink drawing. This method explains the density of line in many of the pictures.

Quite a number of the sketches differ in some small detail or other from the final illustrations which appear in the books, and where they do, these differences are noted and commented upon.

In addition to the sketches originally made between 1926 and 1928, we have also included a number of preliminary drawings for coloured illustrations which Shepard made for later editions of the books, and several other illustrations which will be entirely new to readers, having been omitted from the books in favour of different pictures or because of lack of space.

As Shepard was paid a flat fee for his drawings to *When We Were Very Young* (he received royalties from *Winnie-the-Pooh* onwards), he sold most of his sketches for that book to augment his income, which explains their absence from the Victoria and Albert Museum's collection, and from this book.

Although, of necessity, this is only a selection from the Shepard bequest, it is hoped that it will delight all who love A.A. Milne's Bear of Very Little Brain and who admire the work of the artist who brought him so perfectly to life.

Brian Sibley

POOH & COMPANY

A series of studies 'from life' made in 1924.

'The animals in the stories,' wrote A. A. Milne, 'came for the most part from the nursery . . . Shepard drew them, as one might say, from the living model. They were what they are for anyone to see; I described rather than invented them.'*

A study of Christopher Robin Milne's teddy-bear, Winnie-the-Pooh. However, the bear who appears in the final illustrations was actually modelled on 'Growler' a teddy-bear belonging to Graham Shepard, the artist's son.

Here and on the following page are studies of the original Tigger, Piglet, Kanga, Roo and Eeyore.

*from *It's Too Late Now; The Autobiography of a Writer* by A. A. Milne (Methuen 1939), page 223

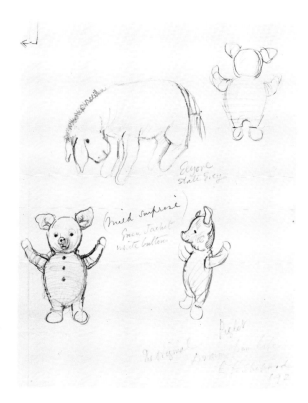

There are no preliminary studies of Owl, but this sketch was made for Chapter 5 of *The House at Pooh Corner*.

All the original toys (with the exception of Roo who got himself lost somewhere in Sussex) are now resident in the New York office of Milne's American publishers, E.P. Dutton & Co.

A study for Rabbit.

'Only Rabbit and Owl,' wrote A.A. Milne, 'were my own
unaided work.'★ Shepard made this study from an exhibit
in the British Museum (Natural History).

★from *It's Too Late Now:*
The Autobiography of a Writer
by A.A. Milne
(Methuen 1939), page 223

Studies of trees.

While preparing his illustrations, Ernest Shepard visited A.A. Milne at his home in Sussex, and together they walked in the Ashdown Forest, 'where I made sketches of the pine trees and the spots that figured in his stories.'★

★from a letter from E.H. Shepard to the Editor dated 23rd October 1969

WHEN WE WERE VERY YOUNG (1924)

Although there are no sketches for *When We Were Very Young* in the Victoria and Albert Museum collection, there are several preliminary drawings for the colour illustrations which Shepard made in 1932 for *The Christopher Robin Verses*.

'Happiness'

'Teddy Bear'

This is the poem which introduced readers to Winnie-the-Pooh, then
known as Mr Edward Bear.

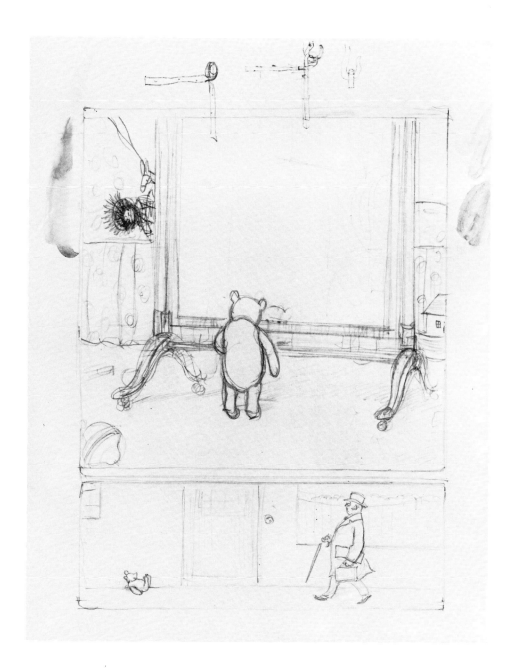

'The Mirror'

A pencil sketch, based on the original illustration in *When We Were Very Young*, possibly made as a preliminary drawing for a colour picture in *The Christopher Robin Verses* but not used.

In his introduction to *When We Were Very Young*, Milne wrote: 'You will find some lines about a swan . . . Christopher Robin, who feeds the swan in the mornings, has given him the name of "Pooh". This is a very fine name for a swan, because, if you call him and he doesn't come (which is a thing swans are good at), then you can pretend that you were just saying "Pooh!" to show how little you wanted him . . .' Then, in his Introduction to *Winnie-the-Pooh*, Milne reminded his readers about 'Pooh' and explained that 'when we said good-bye, we took the name with us, as we didn't think the swan would want it any more. Well, when Edward Bear said that he would like an exciting new name all to himself, Christopher Robin said at once . . . that he was Winnie-the-Pooh. And he was.'

The 'Winnie' part of Bear's new name was borrowed from a famous bear who lived at the London Zoo.

WINNIE-THE-POOH (1926)

Sketch of Christopher Robin's map (used as an end-paper design for
Winnie-the-Pooh). The misspellings are, of course, deliberate;
although in the caption to the published drawing, the 'd' in 'Shepard'
was put back.

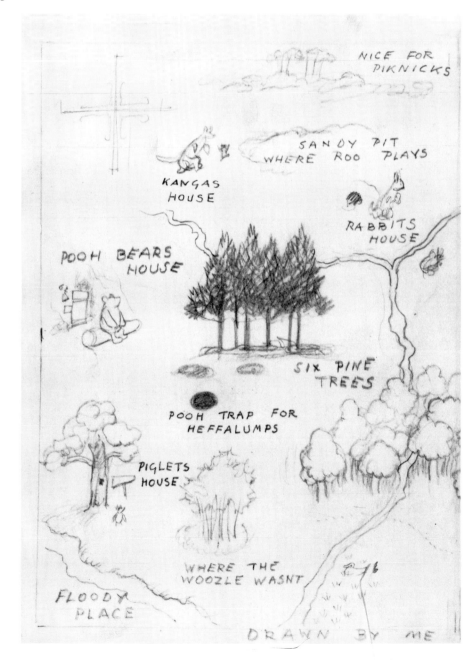

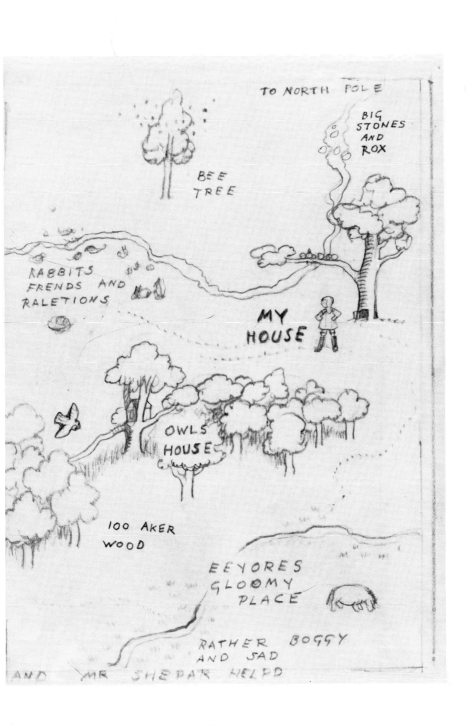

TO NORTH POLE

BIG
STONES
AND
ROX

BEE
TREE

RABBITS
FRENDS AND
RALETIONS

MY
HOUSE

OWLS
HOUSE

100 AKER
WOOD

EEYORES
GLOOMY
PLACE

RATHER BOGGY
AND SAD

AND   MR SHEPAR HELPD

Chapter 1: 'In Which We are Introduced to Winnie-the-Pooh
              and Some Bees, and the Stories Begin'

In the published drawing the bees
follow a less formal flight pattern.

Two studies for the Bee Tree, a
sketch of Pooh climbing it, and
the drawing as published.

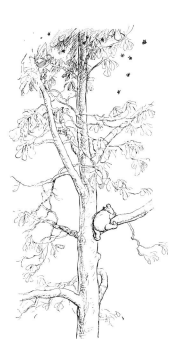

A sketch showing a detail of the larger illustration in which Pooh calls at Christopher Robin's house. In the sketch, Pooh is still stuck with gorse prickles.

The drawing as published

The finished drawing of Pooh
looking at the upside down
BATH MAT (for which this is
a sketch), appears on the page
facing the Introduction.

Chapter 2: 'In Which Pooh Goes Visiting and Gets into a Tight Place.'

Sketch and published drawing
showing Pooh doing his
Stoutness Exercises. Shepard
appears to have first thought of
giving Pooh a mirror such as
that used by Edward Bear in
When We Were Very Young (see
page 16).

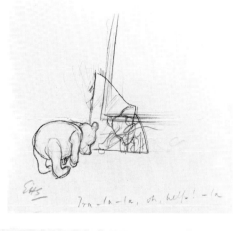

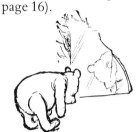

A preliminary sketch for a later coloured illustration of the same
scene used in *The World of Pooh* (1958).

An early sketch of Pooh rum-tum-tum-tiddle-uming his way through the forest (with Rabbit's front door in the foreground), and a detailed sketch for the finished picture (minus the bird which he later added flying overhead).

The drawing as published

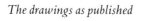

The drawings as published

up hill

Chapter 3: 'In Which Pooh and Piglet Go Hunting and
        Nearly Catch a Woozle'

A series of pictures showing the development of the artist's conception of Piglet's House:

A study of a tree from nature was followed by a preliminary sketch with the 'TRESPASSERS W' notice placed over the door between the tree's roots. This formed the basis for the illustration that was used when the story was previewed in *The Royal Magazine* (July 1926). Lastly the picture as published in the book, in which the notice has been 'moved' to a post on the right of the tree, its original location over the door being indicated by the close cross-hatching on the lower part of the tree.

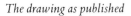

The drawing as published

A rough drawing and a more finished
sketch illustrating the Woozle Hunt.

The drawing as published

Chapter 4: 'In Which Eeyore Loses a Tail and Pooh Finds One'

A first study and a final sketch of Pooh's visit to 'The Chestnuts', Owl's 'old-world residence of great charm.'

The drawing as published

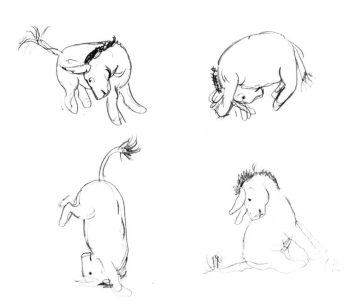

The published drawings of the re-tailed Eeyore
appear in a different order from these sketches.

Chapter 5: 'In Which Piglet Meets a Heffalump'

A sketch for an unpublished picture illustrating the following passage:

'Pooh looked round to see that nobody else was listening, and said in a very solemn voice . . . "I have decided to catch a Heffalump."'

Shepard originally intended these two sketches to appear together, and that is how they were first printed in *The Royal Magazine* (September 1926); however, when the book was published the picture of Pooh was moved to another point in the chapter, and was replaced by the drawing of Pooh lifting up his head 'jar and all', and making 'a loud, roaring noise of Sadness and Despair.'

Chapter 6: 'In Which Eeyore has a Birthday
              and Gets Two Presents'

A small sketch showing a detail
for the illustration of Eeyore
looking at himself in the
stream, and the finished pencil
drawing.

"Sad?" Why should I be sad? "Its my birthday"

This sketch shows Piglet jumping up and down trying to reach the knocker on Pooh's door (as described in the text), and this is how the illustration first appeared in *The Royal Magazine* (August 1926); in the illustration in the book, however, Shepard has added some flower pots for Piglet to stand on.

Chapter 7: 'In Which Kanga and Baby Roo Come to the Forest, and Piglet has a Bath'

In the published illustration, the horizon landscape was omitted, and a flight of birds was added to the left of the trees.

Chap VII
p 96   "Look at me jumping,"
        Kanga + Baby Roo.

An unused sketch of Pooh watching
Kanga going off with Piglet
in her pocket, and (above) the drawing
which was finally used in the book.

This drawing appears to be a preliminary sketch for a coloured illustration (possibly for *The World of Pooh*) which was not used. The tree is the same one which Pooh passed on his way to visit Rabbit (see page 25).

Chapter 8: 'In Which Christopher Robin Leads an Expotition
to the North Pole'

The drawing as published

The sloping perspective given to the procession here was abandoned when the illustration was published in the book (possibly through rearrangement by the printer).

Alexander Beetle going to ground after being 'Hushed' by everyone.

In this sketch, the artist has drawn
Eeyore with several pairs of ears, as he
experimented to find the best position.

The drawing as published

In the published illustration,
Piglet stands on the right of the
picture alongside Kanga.

This appears to be a preliminary
sketch for a later coloured
illustration (possibly for *The
World of Pooh*) which was not
used.

Chapter 9: 'In Which Piglet is Entirely Surrounded by Water'

The drawing as published

A rough drawing and a more
finished sketch showing the
boarding of 'The Brain of
Pooh'.

"Pooh Set in"

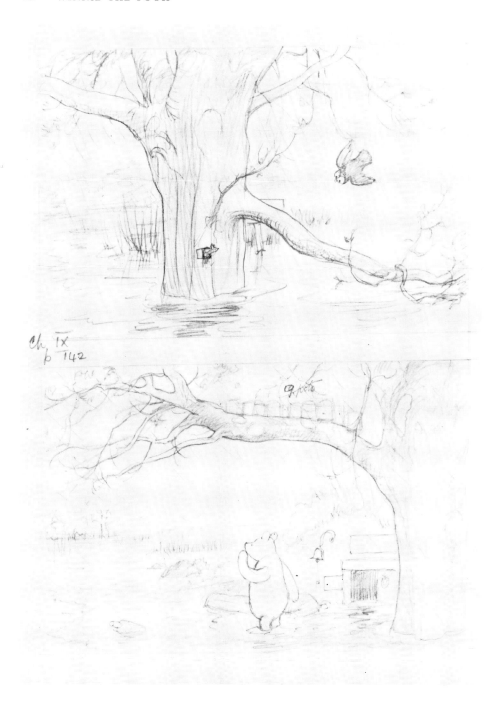

A preliminary sketch for a later coloured illustration in *The World of Pooh* (1958).

Chapter 10: 'In Which Christopher Robin Gives a Pooh Party,
and We Say Good-bye'

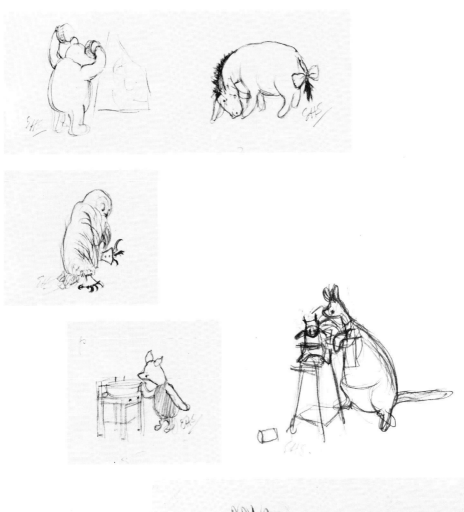

A preliminary sketch for a later
coloured illustration in
The World of Pooh (1958).

The drawing as published

In the published picture,
Piglet, Kanga and Eeyore
can be seen waiting
at the top of the stairs.

NOW WE ARE SIX (1927)

In a postscript to his Introduction, A.A. Milne wrote: 'Pooh wants us to say that he thought it was a different book; and he hopes you won't mind, but he walked through it one day looking for his friend Piglet and sat down on some of the pages by mistake.'

'Solitude'

Preliminary drawing for 'Binker' with unidentified sketch of Pooh.

Three sketches for
illustrations to
'The Charcoal Burner'.

A series of sketches and published illustrations for 'Us Two'.

In the sketch, Pooh is shown looking round a corner of the door; whereas, in the final picture, he appears in the room.

The drawings as published

Two early sketches and the published
illustrations showing Pooh and
Christopher Robin frightening the
'dragons'.

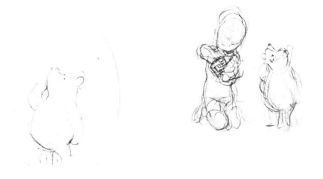

Two unused sketches for the poem.

The published version of this drawing
was reversed in order to conform with
the staircase shown in *Winnie-the-Pooh*
(see pages 20 and 51), and Pooh was
drawn one stair lower down.

A series of sketches for 'The Engineer'.

On the far right can be seen the faint outline of Eeyore's head. He was drawn in full for the published illustration.

The model porter at the end of the platform was omitted from the finished drawing, and Piglet and Kanga were shown carrying their luggage in their right – rather than their left – paws.

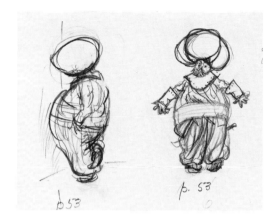

This unused sketch of Pooh and Piglet dancing appears on a sheet of drawings for 'The Emperor's Rhyme', although this seems to have been the result of another of Pooh's mistakes!

'Down by the Pond'

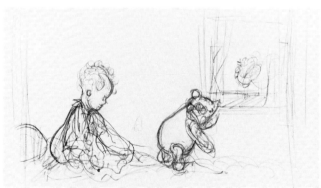

'The Little Black Hen'

Pooh was omitted from the published illustration.

Four sketches for 'The Friend'. Although these illustrations appeared in *The Royal Magazine* (November 1927), they were omitted from the book. In the final version of the picture of Pooh and Christopher Robin whispering, Pooh is shown hiding behind a curtain.

'Look! I told you! Here's the sun!' A sketch for an illustration published in *The Royal Magazine* (September 1927), but omitted from the book.

'Waiting at the Window'

'Forgotten'

The view from the terrace is of Cotchford Farm, the Milnes' house in Sussex.

The drawing as published

An unused sketch of the toys sitting 'five on the high wall and four on the low'.

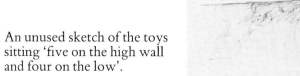

A series of sketches for the poem showing the toys and their young owner 'John boy'. An additional toy, playing cymbals, was added to two of the published illustrations.

The drawing as published

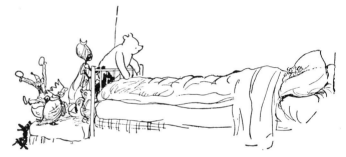

The drawing as published

'The End'

An unused sketch for 'The End', showing
Christopher Robin, Pooh and Piglet in Christopher's
hollow-tree-house at Cotchford Farm.

THE HOUSE AT POOH CORNER (1928)

Sketches for the end-paper design. In the published
drawing, the silhouetted figures process in the opposite
direction; and the character's 'autographs' appear beneath
the picture.

A detail sketch of pine trees, used as part of the
background.

Chapter 1: 'In Which a House is Built at
Pooh Corner for Eeyore'

In the finished illustration,
Piglet holds his stick
in the opposite paw.

In the published drawing,
Piglet climbs down the back
of the gate.

As indicated by the artist's note, the figure
of Pooh was drawn smaller for the final picture.

Chapter 2: 'In Which Tigger Comes to the Forest and has Breakfast'

The drawing as published

Two sketches for
'Tiggers don't like honey'.

A first sketch for the illustration showing Pooh, Piglet and Tigger going to see Eeyore about some breakfast.

A sketch showing the setting for this scene in detail, but omitting Tigger.

A study of pine trees used to replace those in the horizon of the previous sketch.

The drawing as published

He found a small Tin of
Condensed milk!

Chapter 3: 'In Which a Search is Organdized, and
Piglet Meets the Heffalump Again'

Pooh said goodbye affectionately to his fourteen pots of honey

A sketch for a forest background in the
illustration in which Owl and Rabbit
lead the search for Small.

The drawing as published

A study of the tree which Christopher Robin climbs looking for Small.

The drawing as published

Chapter 4: 'In Which it is Shown that Tiggers Don't Climb Trees'

In the finished drawing, Kanga
is shown holding a brush.

Come on Tigger it's easy.

The position in which Christopher Robin stands is different in the published drawing.

Chapter 5: 'In Which Rabbit has a Busy Day,
and We Learn What Christopher Robin
Does in the Mornings'

In the published illustration, Rabbit has his right paw placed thoughtfully to his chin. The snail doorknocker on Christopher Robin's door can be seen rather more clearly than in the final drawing.

Sketch for the illustration of Pooh making up his 'ordinary biggish sort of basket'. In the finished picture Pooh appears rather more in profile.

Chapter 6: 'In which Pooh Invents a New Game
and Eeyore Joins In'

A preliminary sketch for
Poohsticks Bridge – based on
the bridge near Cotchford Farm
– and the published illustration
to which the figures of Pooh,
Piglet, Roo and Rabbit have
been added.

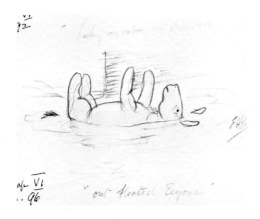

'out floated Eeyore'

A sketch for a later coloured illustration in *The World of Pooh* (1958). The original Poohsticks Bridge does not have a brick arch.

Two sketches (the first not used) showing Christopher Robin 'all sunny and careless . . . just as if twice nineteen didn't matter a bit'.

Chapter 7: 'In Which Tigger is Unbounced'

In the finished illustrations for which these are sketches, the artist shaded the characters and created an impression of mistiness.

Oh! Tigger I am glad to see you
said Rabbit

Chapter 8: 'In Which Piglet Does a Very Grand Thing'

The drawing as published

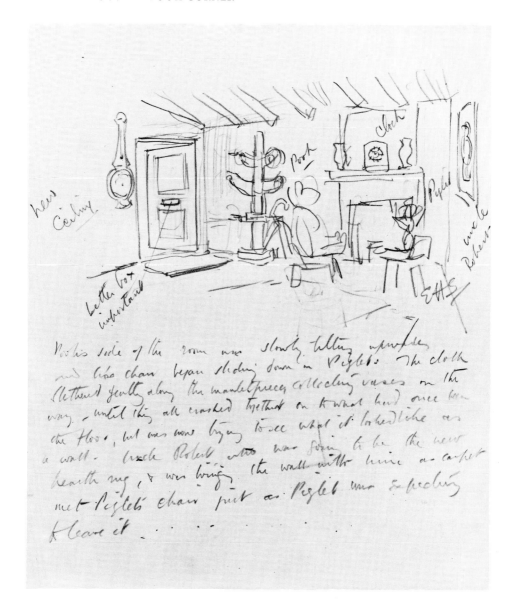

A rough sketch for the interior of Owl's house,
with annotations in the artist's hand.

A VIII
137

Pooh," said owl severely "did you do that"

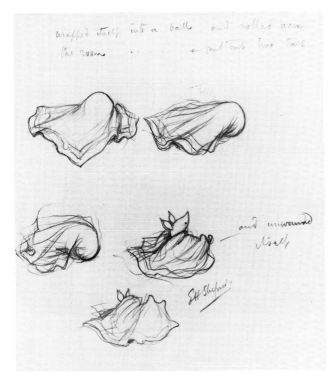

wrapped itself into a ball and rolled across the room . . . . + put out two ears

and unwound itself

E.H. Shepard

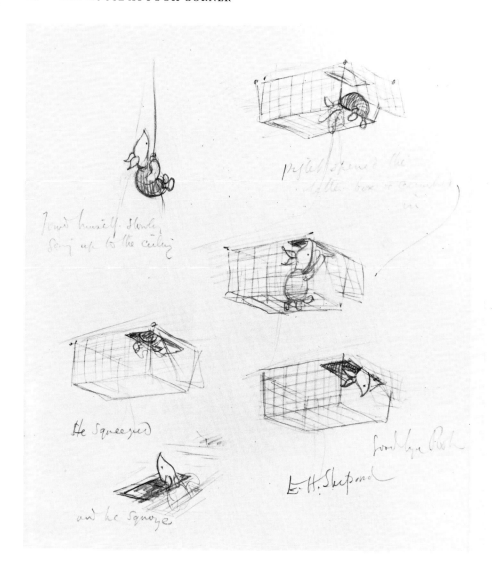

Six sketches of Piglet doing the Very Grand Thing he did,
the third of which (showing him about to climb through
the slit) was omitted from the book.

This drawing appears to have been made as a preliminary sketch for a later coloured picture (possibly for *The World of Pooh*) which was not used. The tree is based on that which Christopher Robin climbs during the search for Small (see page 72).

Chapter 9: 'In Which Eeyore Finds the Wolery
and Owl Moves Into It'

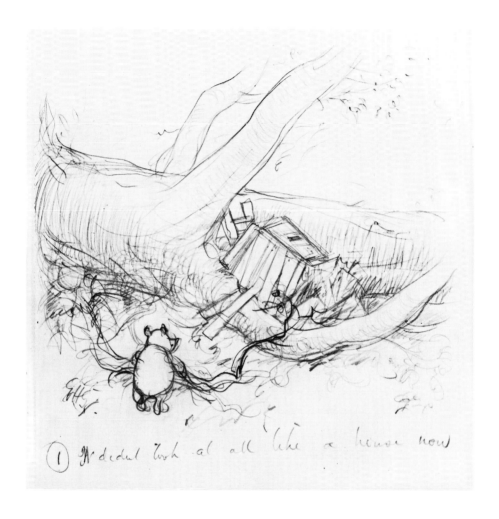

① It didn't look at all like a house now

Chapter 10: 'In Which Christopher Robin and Pooh Come to an Enchanted Place, and We Leave Them There'

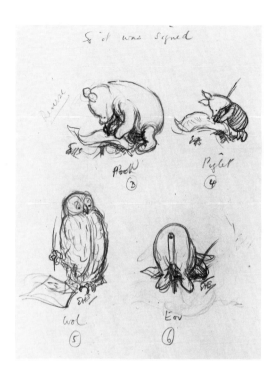

As indicated by the artist's note, the picture of Pooh was finally drawn facing the other way.

In the published illustration, Alexander Beetle was added at the far right of the group.

A Sketch for Galleons Lap, based on Gill's Lap
at the top of the Ashdown Forest.

The drawing as published

A sketch for the coloured dust-wrapper
designed in 1966 for *The Christopher Robin
Story Book* (originally published in 1929).